# Dancing Feet!

by
Lindsey Craig

illustrations by
Marc Brown

Alfred A. Knopf

New York

For Mary and Lucy—my darling dancers!
—L.C.

For Leo Lionni, with considerable admiration
—M.B.

THIS IS A BORZOI BOOK PUBLISHED BY ALFRED A. KNOPF

Text copyright © 2010 by Lindsey Craig
Illustrations copyright © 2010 by Marc Brown

Visit us on the Web! www.randomhouse.com/kids

Educators and librarians, for a variety of teaching tools,
visit us at www.randomhouse.com/teachers

Library of Congress Cataloging-in-Publication Data
Craig, Lindsey.
Dancing feet! / by Lindsey Craig ; illustrated by Marc Brown. — 1st ed.
p.   cm.
Summary: Easy-to-read, rhyming text depicts different animals dancing.
ISBN 978-0-375-86181-9 (trade) — ISBN 978-0-375-96181-6 (lib. bdg.)
[1. Stories in rhyme. 2. Dance—Fiction. 3. Animals—Fiction.]
I. Brown, Marc Tolon, ill. II. Title.
PZ8.3.C84367Dan 2010      [E]—dc22      2009039372

The text of this book is set in 40-point and 60-point Arthur.
The illustrations in this book were created using hand-painted papers and a
collage technique that focused on cutting the paper into primary shapes.

MANUFACTURED IN CHINA
May 2010
10 9 8 7 6 5 4 3 2 1

First Edition

*Tippity! Tippity!*
Little black feet!
Who is dancing
that *tippity* beat?

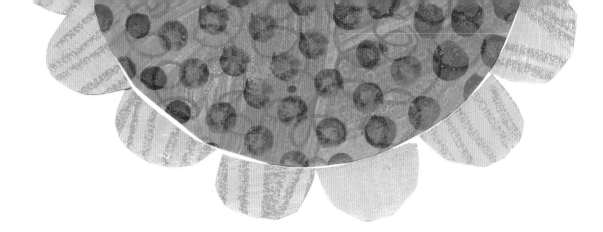

Ladybugs are dancing
on *tippity* feet.
*Tippity! Tippity!*
Happy feet!

Stompity! Stompity!
Big gray feet!
Who is dancing
that *stompity* beat?

Elephant is dancing
on *stompity* feet.
*Stompity! Stompity!*
Happy feet!

*Slappity! Slappity!*
Webbed orange feet!
Who is dancing
that *slappity* beat?

Ducks are dancing
on *slappity* feet.
*Slappity! Slappity!*
Happy feet!

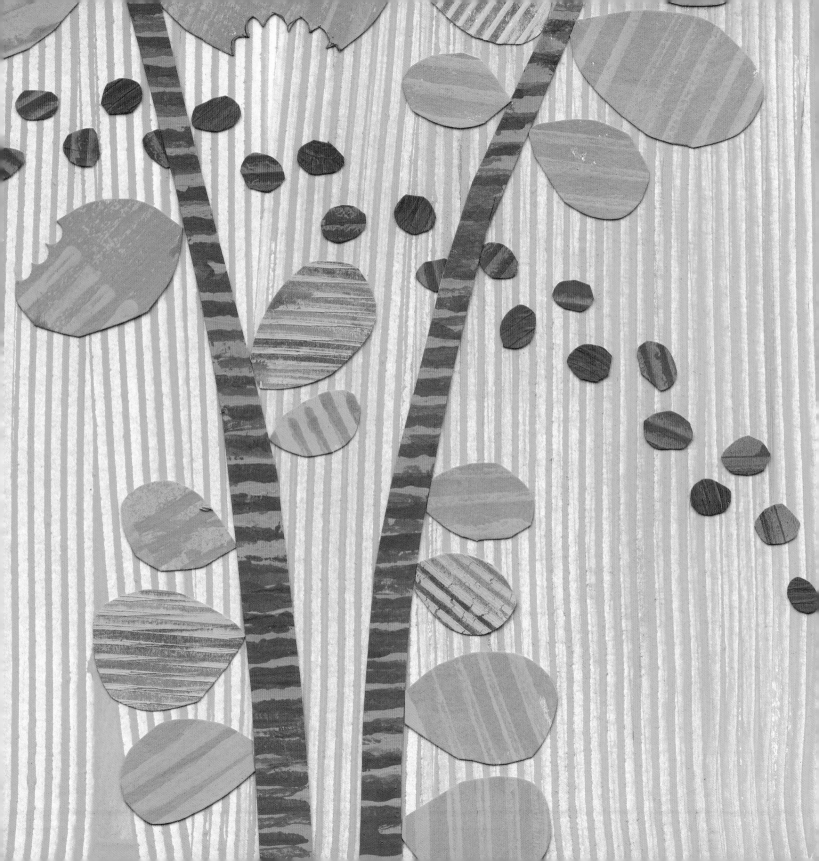

*Creepity! Creepity!*
Lots of purple feet!
Who is dancing
that *creepity* beat?

Caterpillar's dancing
on *creepity* feet.
*Creepity! Creepity!*
Happy feet!

*Thumpity! Thumpity!*
Furry brown feet!
Who is dancing
that *thumpity* beat?

Bear is dancing

on *thumpity* feet.

*Thumpity! Thumpity!*

Happy feet!

*Clickity! Clickity!*
Long green feet!
Who is dancing
that *clickity* beat?

Lizard is dancing

on *clickity* feet.

*Clickity! Clickity!*

Happy feet!

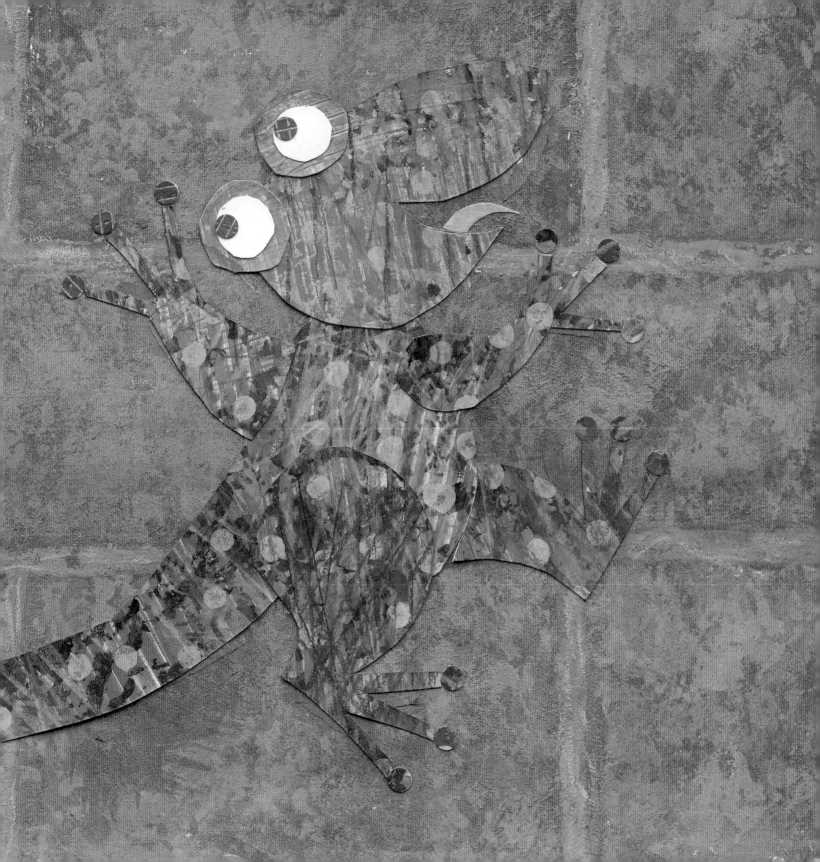

*Stampity! Stampity!*
Hear our feet!
Who is dancing
that *stampity* beat?
We are dancing
on *stampity* feet.
*Stampity! Stampity!*
Happy feet!

*Thumpity!*

*Tippity!*

*Creepity!*

Slappity!

Clickity!

Stompity!

Stampity!

Happy, happy
dancing feet!